Welcome to
Hopscotch Hill School!
In Miss Sparks's class,
you will make friends
with children just like you.
They love school,
and they love to learn!
Keep an eye out for Razzi,
the class pet rabbit.
He may be anywhere!
See if you can spot him
as you read the story.

Avery

Spencer

Nathan

Razzi

Lindy

Delaney

Connor

Published by Pleasant Company Publications
Copyright © 2004 by American Girl, LLC
For information, address:
Book Editor, Pleasant Company Publications, 8400 Fairway Place,
P.O. Box 620998, Middleton, WI 53562.

Visit our Web site at **americangirl.com**.

Printed in China
05 06 07 08 09 10 C&C 10 9 8 7 6

Hopscotch Hill School™ and logo, Hopscotch Hill™,
Where a love for learning grows™, Gwen™, and
American Girl® are trademarks of American Girl, LLC.

Cataloging-in-Publication data available from the Library of Congress

American Girl

GoodSport
Gwen

by Valerie Tripp *illustrated by* Joy Allen

Hurray!

"Go, Gwen, go!"
cheered the children.
It was a bright,
sunny Monday.
Gwen was playing
soccer during recess.
Quick as a flash,
Gwen dribbled the ball down the field.
Whomp! Gwen kicked the ball hard.
Whoosh! The ball flew through the air.
Wham! The ball shot into the goal.
"Hurray!" cheered Gwen's team.
Gwen grinned. She loved to play soccer!
Gwen was the fastest runner,
the hardest kicker,
and the highest scorer on the team.

The game started up again.

Gwen's teammate Delaney had the ball.

A player from the other team

stole the ball from Delaney.

Gwen ran fast.

Quick as a flash, Gwen got the ball back.

Whomp! Gwen kicked the ball.

Whoosh! It flew straight to Delaney.

Wham! Delaney kicked the ball

into the goal.

"Hurray!" cheered the team.

"Way to go, Delaney!"

The bell rang. Recess was over.

Gwen said, "Great game, Delaney.

Our team won because of you."

Delaney grinned.

She said, "No, Gwen. I made that goal

because you passed the ball to me.

You are a good sport.

We won because of YOU."

"Hurray!" cheered the team.

"Hurray for Good Sport Gwen!"

The children went into the classroom.

Connor said to Miss Sparks,

"Gwen helped Delaney score a goal.

Gwen is a good sport."

The sparkles on Miss Sparks's eyeglasses
glittered.

Miss Sparks said, "I am proud of the way
Gwen and Delaney worked together."

"Hurray!" cheered the children.

Miss Sparks pointed to a list of words
on the board.

She said, "Please write these
spelling words in your journals."

Gwen and the other children

wrote the words in their journals.

Miss Sparks said,

"We will study these words all week.

Then on Friday

we will do something new.

We will have a spelling bee."

"Hurray!" cheered the children.

"Buzz," buzzed Spencer.

"B, U, Z, Z.

I'm a bee that can spell.

I'm a spelling bee."

Everyone laughed.

Gwen raised her hand.

She asked,

"How will the spelling bee work?"

Miss Sparks held up a list.

She said, "I have divided our class

into two teams.

Children whose names begin

with a letter from **A** to **K**

are on the blue team.

Children whose names begin

with a letter from **L** to **Z**

are on the red team."

Quick as a flash,

Gwen saw that she was on the blue team.

Miss Sparks said,

"I will ask each one of you to spell a word.

The team that spells the most words

correctly will win the spelling bee."

Gwen was excited. She loved games!

She loved being on a team!

She could not wait for the spelling bee!

Finally Friday came.

Miss Sparks said,

"Red team, line up by the windows.

Blue team, line up by the bulletin board."

Quick as a flash, Gwen lined up

with the blue team.

Miss Sparks said, "Avery, spell **run.**"

Gwen held her breath.

She hoped her teammate Avery

would spell **run** right.

Avery spelled, "**R, U, N.**"

"Correct," said Miss Sparks.

Gwen cheered, "Way to go, Avery!"

Miss Sparks said, "Lindy, spell **hop.**"

Lindy spelled, "**H, O, P.**"

"Correct," said Miss Sparks.

"Hurray!" cheered the red team.

Miss Sparks said, "Gwen, spell **cut.**"

Gwen thought hard.

She was not sure if **cut**

started with a **C** or a **K.**

Gwen spelled slowly, "**C, U, T.**"

"Correct," said Miss Sparks.

"Hurray!" cheered Gwen.

She raised her arms

over her head.

She jumped up and down.

She loved the spelling bee!

Gwen said,

"Hurray for the blue team!

We are going to win!"

All the children on the blue team

cheered, "Hurray!"

Stung by the Spelling Bee

The spelling bee was so exciting!

Now it was the red team's turn.

Miss Sparks said, "Nathan, spell **can.**"

Nathan spelled, "**C, A, N.**"

Miss Sparks said, "Correct."

Then she said, "Delaney, spell **sit.**"

But Delaney was whispering to Hallie. Delaney did not hear Miss Sparks.

Gwen frowned.

Gwen said, "Delaney! It's your turn!"

"Oops!" said Delaney.

"What was my word again?"

Miss Sparks said, "Please spell **sit.**"

Delaney said, "Hmm." She giggled.

Gwen thought Delaney was not trying.

Gwen said, "Come on, Delaney. Try."

Delaney spelled, "**C, I, T.**"

Miss Sparks said, "No, dear, I'm sorry."

Gwen groaned.

Miss Sparks said, "Skylar,

can you spell **sit**?"

Skylar spelled, "**S, I, T.**"

"Correct," said Miss Sparks.

Gwen gulped.

Now the blue team was behind the red team!

Miss Sparks said, "Connor, spell **pen.**"

Connor looked at the ceiling.

Gwen said, "Come on, Connor. That's easy!"

Connor's face turned red.

Connor spelled, "**P, I, N.**"

Miss Sparks said, "No, dear."

Gwen glared at Connor.

Miss Sparks said, "Spencer,

can you spell **pen**?"

Spencer spelled, "**P, E, N.**"

Miss Sparks said, "Correct."

Gwen moaned.

Now the blue team was

even farther behind the red team.

The spelling bee went on and on.

Gwen's teammate Avery

spelled **hat** correctly.

But Hallie spelled **cot** wrong.

Then it was Gwen's turn again.

Miss Sparks said, "Gwen, spell **hit.**"

Gwen was very jittery.

She didn't stop to think.

Quick as a flash,

Gwen spelled, "**H, E, T.**"

Miss Sparks said, "No, dear."

Gwen smacked her forehead.

Miss Sparks said, "Logan,

can you spell **hit**?"

Logan spelled, "**H, I, T.**"

Miss Sparks said, "Yes, that's right.

That was the last word.

The red team wins."

"Hurray!" cheered the red team.

Everyone on the blue team

clapped for the red team, except Gwen.

Gwen frowned.

Gwen said, "We were terrible!"

Delaney shrugged.

She said, "Oh, well. It's no big deal."

Gwen stamped her foot.

Her face was red.

Her voice was angry.

She burst out,

"Our blue team stinks!"

The room was very quiet.

Everyone was surprised at Gwen.

Spencer said to Lindy,

"Gwen is really mad.

She must have been stung

by the spelling bee."

Lindy said, "No one will want to be

on Gwen's team again."

Gwen slumped sadly
at her desk.
She was sorry that she had
acted like a bad sport.
She was sure that her
teammates were unhappy with her.
On Monday Miss Sparks gave the class
a new list of spelling words.
She said, "We will have a spelling bee
with these words on Friday."
The children on the red team smiled.
The children on the blue team frowned.
Gwen blushed.
She knew that everyone
on the blue team was remembering
what a bad sport she had been.

At recess time Gwen stayed inside.

Miss Sparks said, "Gwen,

why aren't you playing soccer today?"

Gwen hung her head.

She said, "I don't think anyone

wants to play with me.

I was mean about

the spelling bee

last week.

Now everyone thinks

that I am a bad sport."

Miss Sparks said,

"I don't think so.

You helped Delaney at soccer.

That's what good sports do.

They help their teammates do well."

25

Gwen said, "But spelling isn't like soccer.

I can't help my teammates in spelling."

Miss Sparks said, "Are you sure?"

Miss Sparks thought for a moment.

She asked, "How did your soccer team

get to be so good?"

Gwen said, "We practiced a lot."

"Ah," said Miss Sparks.

"You practiced."

Gwen perked up.

She said, "I have

a great idea!

I will help my

spelling bee team.

I will find a way for us

to practice our spelling words."

26

Miss Sparks smiled.

She said, "That is a good idea."

Gwen smiled too. She said,

"The blue team will practice spelling.

And I will practice being a good sport.

I won't get stung

by the spelling bee again!"

Gwen's Great Game

The next day was Tuesday.

Gwen hurried outside at recess.

She said, "Hey, blue team!"

Avery, Connor, Delaney, and Hallie

looked at Gwen.

Gwen said, "I am sorry about

the way I acted after the spelling bee.

I hope you will forgive me.

I made up a game

to help us practice spelling.

Please play it with me."

The children looked at one another.

They were not sure that they wanted

to play Gwen's game.

But Delaney said,

"Tell us about your game, Gwen."

Gwen said, "We stand in a line

facing the soccer goal.

I pass the ball to you and

call out a word.

If you spell the word right,

you kick the ball into the goal.

If you do not spell the word right,

you run to the end of the line."

The blue team said, "Let's play!"

They lined up facing the soccer goal.

Gwen passed the ball to Delaney.

Gwen said, "Spell **dog.**"

Delaney spelled, "**D, O, G.**"

"Right!" cheered the children.

Whomp! Delaney kicked the ball hard.

Whoosh! The ball flew through the air.

Wham! The ball shot into the goal.

Delaney passed the ball to Connor.

She said, "Spell **get.**"

Connor spelled, "**G, I, T.**"

"Oops!" said the children. "That's wrong."

Quick as a flash, Connor ran

to the end of the line.

The blue team played Gwen's game

all during recess.

Whomp! Whoosh! Wham!

The children called out words to spell.

They kicked and ran and laughed.

They spelled and spelled and spelled.

The blue team played

Gwen's game on Wednesday

and Thursday too.

Whomp! Whoosh! Wham!

They practiced their spelling words
over and over again.

They loved playing Gwen's great game!

At last it was Friday.

Miss Sparks said, "Boys and girls,
it is time for our spelling bee."

"Hurray!" cheered all the children.

Gwen smiled at her teammates.

"Okay, blue team," she said. "Ready?"

"Yes!" said the blue team.

Miss Sparks said, "Delaney, spell **sat.**"

Gwen saw Delaney take a deep breath.

Gwen knew that Delaney was trying hard.

Delaney spelled, "**S, A, T.**"

Miss Sparks said, "Correct."

Gwen cheered, "Way to go, Delaney!"

Delaney smiled a big smile.

Miss Sparks said, "Spencer, spell **rug.**

Spencer spelled, "**R, U, G.**"

Miss Sparks said, "Correct."

"Hurray!" cheered the red team.

Miss Sparks said, "Connor, spell **bag.**"

Connor thought hard.

Gwen said, "Take your time, Connor."

Slowly Connor spelled, "**B, A, G.**"

Miss Sparks said, "Correct."

"Hurray!" cheered the blue team.

Gwen jumped up and down.

She cheered, "Way to go, Connor!"

The spelling bee went on.

Gwen and the rest
of the blue team
spelled most of
their words correctly.
The children on
the red team
did too.

35

Gwen cheered whenever someone

on the blue team spelled a word right.

When someone spelled a word wrong,

Gwen said, "That's okay!"

Gwen was so busy cheering

that she was surprised

when Miss Sparks said,

"That was the last word."

Gwen held her breath.

Miss Sparks said,

"There were 20 words in the spelling bee.

The blue team spelled 9 words correctly.

The red team spelled 11 words correctly.

The red team wins."

"Hurray!" cheered the red team.

The blue team looked at Gwen nervously.

Was she going to be a bad sport again?

But Gwen grinned.

Now she knew that good sports

win every time,

no matter what the score is.

She said, "That's okay, blue team.

We will do better next time."

Miss Sparks said,

"You did much better THIS time,

blue team."

Avery said, "That is because

of Gwen's game."

Logan asked, "What is that?"

Everyone on the blue team smiled.

Connor said, "It is a great game that

Gwen made up to practice spelling."

Everyone on the red team said,

"Can we play Gwen's great game too?"

"Sure!" said Gwen.

The sparkles on Miss Sparks's

eyeglasses glittered.

She said, "I am proud of you, Gwen."

Gwen raised her arms over her head.

"Hurray!" she cheered.

She was glad to be

Good Sport Gwen again.

Dear Parents . . .

Just like Gwen, your child is learning to be a good teammate—even if she never kicks a ball or wears a uniform—because she is a member of many groups. Some groups are formal and have lots of members, such as Scouts or choir. Other groups are spontaneous and small, such as the children who want to play Hopscotch at recess or eat at the same lunch table.

Whether the members number two or twenty, your child wants to be an outstanding, understanding member in good standing of all the groups she's in. It is within those groups that she learns how to win with good grace, lose with good humor, and bounce back from disappointment—ready to try again.

How can you cheer your child on to good sportsman-ship? Try the following suggestions for fun at home and at the game. Your child will discover that good sports *always* win, no matter what the score is.

All Sorts of Good Sports

You can coach your child in everyday ways to be a good sport. Encourage her to try new things, always give her best shot, and focus more on *fun* than on what she sees on the scoreboard.

• There are all sorts of good sports in *Good Sport Gwen.* Ask your child to **try to spy** times when other characters in the story show **good sportsmanship.** When is Connor complimentary? How is Miss Sparks a help? When is Delaney forgiving? Chat about how those acts represent good sportsmanship even though they don't happen during sports events.

• Good sports are open to trying new things, even things they may not be very good at yet. Encourage your child to **give new activities a whirl**—without any expectations of perfection. Give her enough time to start over if she wants to and enough materials to transform her mistakes into successes. Congratulate her for a great first-time try!

- **Put fun first.** When you play games with your child, don't keep score. Or try tallying points with a twist, such as giving points to the fastest, funniest, or friendliest player. You might decide before a game that the loser will choose the next game that you play— or the snacks you'll share when the game's over.

- As a pregame warmup, help your child **set a personal goal,** one that's a healthy stretch but not tied to overall performance. Maybe her goal for the game is not to be the high scorer but to stay in her position. Her goal for the ballet recital may be to remember to smile, even if she doesn't perform every step perfectly. Afterward, ask her, "Did you try your best?" and "What was your favorite part?"

- Lead the cheering when your child is a **cheerleader for someone else.** Involve her in making a dessert or planning a party to celebrate her brother's good grade on a test. Can she make him a blue ribbon or a certificate of success? When good sports shine the spotlight on others, they go with the glow!

Go, Team, Go!

Being part of an athletic team is a great way for your child to work with others toward a common goal—which doesn't have to be The Big Win. Don't just cheer from the sidelines! Team up with your child to help her be Number One at supporting her teammates.

• Choosing up sides has its downside: children's feelings are hurt if they're overlooked or chosen last. Have a huddle with your child, and **brainstorm fun and fair ways of forming teams.** Maybe one team is made up of children with birthdays from January through June, and the other of children with birthdays from July through December. Your child can think up lots of ways to write the roster.

- Bring balloons to team practice one day and, just for fun, have the children play **Balloon Ball.** See if they can all work together to keep a balloon in the air throughout the length of a song or until you blow the whistle. Encourage your child to create other cooperative games, where there are no winners or losers—only champions at having fun!

- Ask your child to draw a team picture of a group she belongs to. Ask her how **each member contributes to the team.** Who cheers the loudest for her teammates? Who's the MVP when it comes to comforting other players when they're tired or discouraged? Who tries hard from the start until she crosses the finish line? Help your child identify how she contributes to team spirit, too.

- And what about you? Why not make it your claim to fame that you **stay sane at the game?** Make it a habit to cheer for every good play—including those the other team makes. Cheer the referee for her hard work and effort, too. How about bringing enough snacks for both teams and congratulating all players after the game? You'll be setting a gold-medal example for your child if you do.

Bouncing Back

Striking out, being in a different class from her best friend at school, not getting a part in the school play—your child experiences many disappointments on and off the playing field. You can't make everything work out the way she wants it to, but you can help her work out her feelings and bounce back with renewed energy, enthusiasm, and confidence.

- Just listen. After a defeat or disappointment, **let your child blow off steam** and express her frustration for a while. Acknowledge her feelings. Then help her cool herself down by encouraging her to take deep breaths, count to ten, or do *lemon squeezes*—clenching and then relaxing her fists.

- Suggest to your child that she make a **Feel Better Box,** where she stores drawings of favorite activities on index cards. Encourage her to look through her box when she feels unhappy and choose an activity that makes her feel better. Does playing with her pet cheer her up? Does reading distract and refresh her? Does a bubble bath wash her worries away? Remind her that if one activity doesn't work, she can try another. When she's smiling again, praise her for taking responsibility for turning her feelings around.

- Look ahead. We can't control what happens, but we can control how we react to what happens. **Playact** with your child some ways she might react the next time things get hard. Brainstorm things she could do now to sharpen her skills and **to be ready for the next game**—practicing with her big sister, asking a friend to play with her at recess at school, or watching another team for pointers, ideas, and inspiration.

- Get cozy and **read books** with your child that show her other children who bounce back from disappointments. Ask your child why she thinks that Good Sport Gwen wasn't upset about losing the second spelling bee, even after all the hard work her team put toward practicing the words. Chat about the importance of friendship and how it allows you to enjoy the fun of playing together—even when you don't win.

This story and the "Dear Parents" activities were developed with guidance from the Hopscotch Hill School advisory board:

Dominic Gullo is a professor of Early Childhood Education at Queens College, City University of New York. He is a member of the governing board of the National Association for the Education of Young Children, and he is a consultant to school districts across the country in the areas of early childhood education, curriculum, and assessment.

Margaret Jensen has taught beginning reading for 32 years and is currently a math resource teacher in the Madison Metropolitan School District, Wisconsin. She has served on committees for the International Reading Association and the Wisconsin State Reading Association, and has been president of the Madison Area Reading Council. She has presented at workshops and conferences in the areas of reading, writing, and children's literature.

Kim Miller is a school psychologist at Stephens Elementary in Madison, Wisconsin, where she works with children, parents, and teachers to help solve—and prevent—problems related to learning and adjustment to the classroom setting.

Virginia Pickerell has worked with teachers and parents as an educational consultant and counselor within the Madison Metropolitan School District. She has researched and presented workshops on topics such as learning processes, problem solving, and creativity. She is also a former director of Head Start.